I Like Me!

by Deborah Connor Coker
illustrated by Keaf Holliday

*This Little Golden Storybook™ was published
in cooperation with Essence Communications, Inc.*

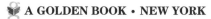

A GOLDEN BOOK • NEW YORK
Golden Books Publishing Company, Inc., New York, New York 10106

My mom says I'm the color of all the leaves in the fall.

My dad says that my smile is as bright as sunshine.

I'm Nia Natasha Sierra Sims and I like me.

I have long legs that run fast races . . .

and leap high up in the air.

I have strong arms that give big, happy hugs . . .

and gentle hands that model soft clay.

I have soft fingers to string cat's cradle . . .

and play ten piano keys at once.

I'm Nia Natasha Sierra Sims and I like me.

I have ears that hear stories Grandad tells . . .

and teeth that nibble sweet corn from cobs.

I have a nose that smells sweet mint in leaves . . .

and eyes that see shapes in the sky.

I'm Nia Natasha Sierra Sims and I like me.

I have plans to visit far-off places and discover things no one else has seen.
I have ideas I can share and many more yet to be.

When I get big, I'll surprise the world with all I do.
But I won't surprise me!